Six Months in the Same Boots!

Author and Illustrator
Claire Boggs

Dedication:

To all children without
families, waiting to be chosen.

Six Months in the Same Boots is a story based on a true story of 2 little boys waiting for their forever families. Their future is in God's hands. One boy was adopted and the other boy disappeared.

My husband, Larry, and I have been missionaries in Guatemala for many years. We have had the privilege of helping hundreds of families adopt children internationally.

Along with *Special Delivery International Inc. Adoptions Service*, our motto is:

"Uniting Families with Children and Children with Families"

I would like to thank Larry for encouraging me to write this story for children to read—that they might know God loves them and that He is in control of their lives, too.

Claire Boggs
Author & Illustrator

Gilbert and Terry became good friends at the new orphanage in Guatemala, Central America. Gilbert was only six years old. Terry was ten. The boys went to the same school. They shared toys and a bedroom. They liked to play outside and they loved to watch cartoons together.

Gilbert went to Sunday School with the other children at the Home. Terry had only been to church a couple of times. Terry did not like to sit still and listen. When he was asked to be quiet, Terry just made more noise.

Terry would also sneak around the house and find things to do that were not nice. He would hit the girls. He would take toys away from the little children just to hear them cry, and he would steal sweets from the kitchen when Mama Clarita was not looking. Terry did not like the rules of the house. He didn't like anyone to tell him what to do.

Gilbert, however, knew it was wrong to lie and he knew it was wrong to hit, and he knew it was wrong to take things that belonged to other people, but Gilbert liked Terry. Terry was funny and Gilbert liked to laugh.

Like all little boys who look up to older boys, Gilbert looked up to Terry.

One day Terry was given some really neat, brown, cowboy boots. They were not brand new, but they were still very nice. Terry was lucky, he did not have to tie his shoes when he wore the cowboy boots. Gilbert wished he had boots like Terry's, but at the Children's Home there were no cowboy boots in Gilbert's size. This made him very sad.

One night, Terry was especially mean to Gilbert's sister. He took away her crayons and scribbled on the wall. Then he told Mama Clarita that the little girl had done it. When Gilbert's sister cried and told on Terry, he got in trouble for being so mean.

"No television for one week," said Mama Clarita. "You can't watch cartoons for a week. Terry you need to learn to be nice to others."

Terry went to his room and pouted. He was really mad. He did not like being punished. All night he thought of how he could get even with the little girl and with Mama Clarita.

The next morning he planned his escape. He would wake up, get ready for school, and eat breakfast just as he did every day. (The pancakes at the home were very good.) After eating, he would pretend that he was going to school. Instead, he would sneak out the back door and run away.

That morning, Gil had a question for Terry. "Please, can I wear your cowboy boots today?" Gil begged, "Pleeeease?" Terry did not like to share, but this day he didn't care, he was out of there. Terry wanted to wear his tennis shoes since they were better for running.

"OK, Gil! You can wear the boots today, but they are really too big for you. You will fall down in them, for sure." "Not me, Terry. I'm almost seven," said Gilbert, as he pulled them on. "Look! My toes almost reach the end," said Gil. "These are only a size three and I wear a size one. That's just two sizes bigger," Gil explained.

Gilbert tucked his jeans inside the boots so that everyone could see that he was wearing cowboy boots. He felt so proud.

Clomp! Clomp! Clomp! Gil marched around the Home. "Wow, these boots are really great," Gilbert told Terry. "You are my best friend!"

"I've never had a real friend before," thought Terry, as the boys ate their pancakes. Even though he was happy about having a friend, Terry was still mad that he could not watch cartoons. He was still upset that the little girl had told on him.

Then Terry had a mean thought. Since the little girl was Gil's sister, he could really get back at her if Gilbert were to run away with him. "That would serve her right!" Terry thought.

"Hey, Gil," Terry said in a whisper. "You want to go with me today? I'm heading to the city and you can come with me if you want." "But we have to go to school today," Gil replied. "I'm not going to school today," Terry said. "If you want to come along, I'll let you; but you can't tell anyone and you can't cry."

Gil thought about it for a while. He felt so big with Terry's cowboy boots on. He felt he could do just about anything. "OK," he said, "Let's go!"

"¡Adios!" "¡Vamos a la escuela!"* they lied, sneaking out the backdoor. Terry and Gil took the shortcut and climbed the fence and ran down to the road, going in the same direction as the school. Instead of going to school, Terry waved his hand downward as people do in Guatemala when they are asking for a ride in the back of a pick-up.

*In Spanish "¡Adios!" means, "Good bye!"
"¡Vamos a la escuela!" means, "We are going to school!"*

Soon a man offered them a ride. Gilbert was so excited. He liked riding in the back of the pick-up. Then Terry told another lie. He said to the man driving the pick-up, "I have to go to the city to find my parents." Of course, the sad truth was that Terry did not have parents to take care of him.

Before Terry arrived at the Children's Home, he slept in doorways, on the street. He begged for food and stole fruit from the market. He did not have anyone to tell him right from wrong. Terry was not used to anyone telling him what to do. "Nobody is the boss of me!" he thought.

Off went Terry and Gilbert in the back of the pick-up, along with the pigs, bananas, and vegetables—the wind blowing through their hair. "What an adventure!" they said. "This is really fun!" Gil exclaimed.

The man in the pick-up thought it was strange that two little boys were out so early by themselves. He took them to the city, but he also took them directly to another Children's Home. "¡Adios!" said the man, as he gave them each some money and left them at the Children's Home. "Be good!" he said, as he left.

Gil and Terry did not want to stay at this Children's Home. Instead, they just climbed the fence again and ran away. Now, the boys were hungry, but instead of buying food, they spent the money the man had given them on two watches. A blue watch for Gil and a black one for Terry. "Boy," they thought. "We are best friends."

Since they had no money for food, they decided to steal so they could eat. This was not a good way to live. Gilbert always felt hungry and sad, and the boots were making terrible blisters on his feet.

"I want to go back to the Home," Gilbert said to Terry one day. "I don't like living on the street. I liked my bed. I liked going to school. And my sister is going to worry about me."

"Cry baby!" said Terry. "I told you if you came along, you couldn't cry." Nothing Terry said helped. Gilbert still wanted to go home. The cowboy boots had become very heavy and they hurt his feet.

Just then Gil saw a bus that he remembered would take him to his grandmother's house. Since he was so young, he did not have to pay to ride the bus. He jumped on the bus and never saw Terry again.

Gilbert's grandmother lived in a little, old house with boards in the windows, a dirt floor, and no bathroom. She had no bed. They had to sleep on bags of sand or make beds out of cement blocks and cardboard boxes.

Even so, his grandmother was happy that Gilbert had found his way to her house. The only means she had for making money was to pick up pop cans and guard cars parked on the street. She did not have enough food to eat three times a day. She did not have pancakes with syrup as they did at the Children's Home.

Gilbert really wanted to go back to the Home where things were nice. He remembered the good times: a soft warm bed, hot baths, his sister, school, television, and pancakes.

Six months in the same cowboy boots was no longer fun. Gilbert was tired of those old boots. "Why did I let Terry trick me into leaving?" he asked himself. He had been happy at the Home. There, he had been waiting for a "forever family." Gilbert remembered his happy hours in Sunday School. He remembered the good things he had learned. Gilbert began to pray.

Mama Clarita and his sister were also praying. They prayed for Gilbert every day. They prayed that God would keep him safe and that someday they would find him.

Each time Mama Clarita went to the big city, she would look for Gilbert. "A little boy with big, brown cowboy boots!" she thought. "He should not be too hard to find." Gilbert's sister went to the city twice to try and remember where they had once lived. "Maybe that's where he went," she thought. The little girl just could not remember where they had lived.

Then one evening, Mama Clarita went to the store where Gilbert's Gramma guarded cars in the parking lot. She saw an old woman sitting near a car. "I wonder if that could be Gilbert's Gramma," she thought.

Mama Clarita spoke to the lady and asked if she had a grandson named, Gilbert. Her face lit up as she said, "Yes! And he is at my house!" The next day Mama Clarita went to Gramma's house to find a sad, dirty, little boy standing there, still wearing those same old boots!

"Gilbert, do you want to come back home?"
Mama Clarita asked. "Yes," said Gilbert, giving
Mama Clarita a big hug and smile. "I'm sorry for
running away with Terry!" "That's Ok," said Mama
Clarita. "God forgives us, all, when we are sorry."
She said. "Let's go buy you some new clothes to
go home in. And maybe you would like some new
cowboy boots?" "*No gracias,** I don't want to ever
wear cowboy boots again!"

*In Spanish "No gracias" means, No thank you.

To Parents:

The Bible tells us that Jesus saves.

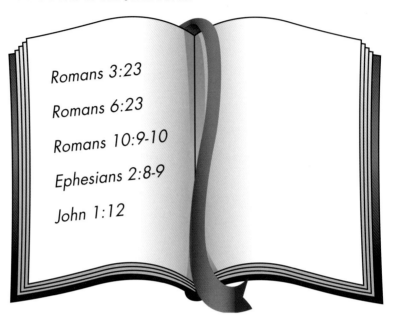

Romans 3:23

Romans 6:23

Romans 10:9-10

Ephesians 2:8-9

John 1:12

Six Months in the Same Boots!

First Edition

Copyright © 2004 by **Mama Clarita Stories**

Library of Congress Control Number 2004108327

ISBN 0-9755283-1-9

Graphic Design & Book Layout by Larry G. Nichols II
Printed in the U.S.A. by **Mennonite Press, Inc.**, Newton, Kansas